HuNgry BirD

JEREMY TANKARD

Scholastic Press **New York**

Bird and his friends

had just set out on a hike

when Bird's tummy rumbled.

"I'm getting hungry," said Bird.
"I might need something to eat."

The other animals didn't answer.
They were too busy enjoying the hike.

"Hey, Fox," said Bird. "Did you pack anything for me to eat? I'm a bit peckish."

"I brought some yummy berries. Would you like a few?"
"No, thanks," said Bird. "Berries are not my favorite."
"Suit yourself," said Fox.

Bird's tummy rumbled louder.

"Hey, Beaver," said Bird. "Have you brought anything delicious to eat? I'm hungry."

"I have lots of nice, crunchy sticks," said Beaver. "Would you like some?"

"Sticks?" said Bird.
"Are you crazy?
   Birds don't eat sticks!"
"Well, beavers do.
   Yum!" said Beaver.

Bird's legs were growing weak.

"Hey, Sheep," said Bird. "Have YOU packed anything tasty? I'm starving."

"I packed some delicious grass," said Sheep. "We could share it!"

"GRASS?" said Bird. "I think you mean GROSS! Who wants to eat GRASS?!"

"I do," said Sheep.
"It's scrumptious!"

Bird could not go one more step.
"Hey, Raccoon!" said Bird. "Please tell
me YOU'VE remembered what I like to eat.
I'm RAVENOUS!"
"I have this nice sandwich," said
Raccoon. "Would you like half?"
"SANDWICH?" said Bird.
"YUCK! That sounds
DISGUSTING!"

"It isn't," said Raccoon.
"It's a medley of flavors."

Bird was sure he was going to pass out from hunger.
"Hey, Rabbit!" shouted Bird. "Give me something
to eat! **NOW!**"

"How about a carrot?" said Rabbit. "Carrots are delicious!"
"CARROTS ARE ORANGE!" shouted Bird.
"HOW ON EARTH CAN I EAT A CARROT?!"

"You crunch it,"
said Rabbit.
"Like this."
CRUNCH, CRUNCH.

Bird's tummy roared and

he collapsed on the ground.

He lay where he had fallen.

He lay there some more.

"You mean NONE of you packed me a snack that I like?" Bird called to his friends.

Bird's friends had stopped to rest on a log
and eat their snacks. They called to him.
Bird could hardly hear them over his noisy tummy.

"BE QUIET, TUMMY," whimpered Bird.
"I'M STARVING TO DEATH HERE!"

Bird looked at his friends happily
munching away.
He was too hungry to walk.
He crawled over to them.

"Okay, fine. I'll try your snacks," said Bird.
He tasted some berries. "These taste very round."
He nibbled some sticks. "Crunchy!"
He chewed some grass. "I feel like a sheep!"

Bird tried the sandwich. "It's not as disgusting as I thought."
He even ate a carrot. "Hmmm, not bad. It DOES taste orange. But I like it!"

Just then Fox spotted something wriggling in the grass.

"BIRD!" he said. "Your favorite snack — a WORM!"

"No thanks," said Bird. "I'm thirsty.
Who brought me a drink?"